Franklin and the Magic Show

From an episode of the animated TV series *Franklin,*
produced by Nelvana Limited, Neurones France s.a.r.l. and
Neurones Luxembourg S.A., based on the Franklin books
by Paulette Bourgeois and Brenda Clark.

Story written by Sharon Jennings

Illustrated by Sean Jeffrey, Alice Sinkner and Shelley Southern

Based on the TV episode *Franklin the Fabulous,* written
by Paula Butorac

ISBN 0-439-41803-8

12 11 10 9 8 7 6 5 4 3 2 1   2 3 4 5 6 7/0

Printed in the U.S.A.   24

First Scholastic printing, September 2002

Edited by Tara Walker
Designed by Stacie Bowes

Franklin and the Magic Show

SCHOLASTIC INC.

New York Toronto London Auckland Sydney
Mexico City New Delhi Hong Kong Buenos Aires

Franklin can tie his shoes.

Franklin can count by twos.

But Franklin cannot disappear.

This is a problem because

Franklin wants to be a magician.

One day, Franklin saw

a magic show.

Marten the Magnificent

did lots of tricks.

He turned a flower into a bird.

He made a chair rise up in the air.

He even made himself disappear.

"Wow!" said Franklin.

"I want to be a magician!"

Franklin ran home.

He found a hat

under his desk.

He found a cape

in his closet.

He found a magic wand

behind his toy box.

He found a book

of magic tricks on his shelf.

"Now I look like a magician,"

said Franklin.

"Now I can put on a magic show."

Franklin went to show his parents.

"I am Franklin the Fabulous,"

he told them.

"You look like a magician,"

said his mother.

"What tricks can you do?"

asked his father.

"I can disappear," said Franklin.

"That's a hard trick,"

said his father.

"Not for me," said Franklin.

Franklin went to find his friends.

"Is it Halloween?"

asked Bear.

"No," said Franklin.

"I am Franklin the Fabulous.

I am putting on a magic show.

You must pay one cookie to watch."

"I'll come," said Bear.

"I'll come," said Beaver.

"We'll all come,"

said everyone.

Franklin ran home to get ready.

Soon his friends came

with their cookies.

Franklin took a bow.

"I am Franklin the Fabulous,"

he said.

Then he waved his magic wand.

Everyone clapped.

"Now I will disappear,"

said Franklin.

"Ohhh!" said everyone.

Franklin got into a big box.

"Count to ten," he told his friends.

"Then open the box."

17

Franklin closed
the lid.
It was dark
inside the box.

"ONE! TWO! THREE!"
said Franklin's friends.
Franklin pushed
on the back
of the box.

"FOUR! FIVE! SIX!"

said Franklin's friends.

Franklin pushed

and pushed.

"SEVEN! EIGHT! NINE!"

said Franklin's friends.

Franklin could not

sneak out the

back of the box.

It was stuck.

"TEN!" said Franklin's friends.

They opened up the box.

"You did not disappear,"

said Beaver.

"I'm going home."

"Me too," said Fox.

"Me too," said Bear. "And I'm

taking my cookie."

"Me too," said everyone.

Franklin went to his room.

"I am not a magician,"

he told his mother.

"I am not Franklin the Fabulous,"

he told his father.

"I am just Franklin,

and I cannot disappear."

"That's a hard trick,"

said his father.

"I can show you an easy trick."

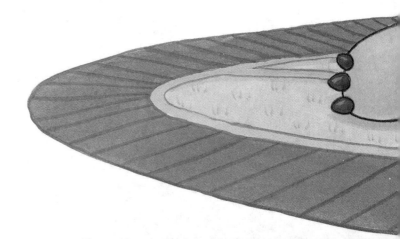

Franklin's father held a penny
in his left hand.

Then he closed both of his hands.

"Where's the penny?" he asked.

Franklin pointed to his left hand.

His father opened his right hand.

In it was the penny.

"Ta dah!" said Franklin's father.

"Wow!" said Franklin.

Franklin's father opened his left hand.

He had a penny in that hand, too.

"You have two pennies!"

cried Franklin.

"I tricked you," said his father.

"That was an easy trick,"

said Franklin.

"I know lots of easy tricks,"

said his father.

"Hmmm," said Franklin.

The next day,

Franklin got out his hat,

his cape and his magic wand.

He went to find his friends.

"I am Franklin the Fabulous,"

he said.

"I am putting on a magic show.

I will give you each a cookie

if you come."

"I'll come," said Bear.

"I'll come," said Beaver.

"We'll all come," said everyone.

Franklin the Fabulous

put on a very good magic show.

He did lots of easy tricks,

but he did not try to disappear.

Only one thing disappeared ...

... the cookies.